BAREFOOT BEAR
AND THE DRAGON

ISBN 0-8300-0338-X

Barefoot Bear and the Dragon
was prepared and produced
by Tern Enterprises, Inc.
Sagaponack Road
Bridgehampton, New York 11932

Cover and book design by Duncan S. McKenzie

Color separations
by Hong Kong Scanner Craft Company Ltd.

Printed and bound in Hong Kong
by Leefung-Asco Printers Ltd.

Barefoot Bear™ is a trademark of
Tern Enterprises, Inc., Bridgehampton, New York

Produced exclusively for **Kaleidoscope**

BAREFOOT BEAR AND THE DRAGON

by Ann Matthews
Illustrated by Cathy Beylon

KALEIDOSCOPE

Barefoot Bear was having a bad day. At dinner he poured himself a glass of milk.

"Be careful, dear," warned his mother.

"I will," said Barefoot. But the milk spilled all over the table.

After dinner, Barefoot's friend Marshall came over to play catch. He threw a low ball to Barefoot. Barefoot dove for it—and missed.

"Mom!" he cried. "I skinned my knee!"

"Oh, Barefoot," said his mother. "Maybe you'd better play inside now."

Barefoot got out his blocks. He began to build a castle. He made a tall tower and a courtyard and a drawbridge over a moat.

Barefoot sat back to admire his work. He felt very proud of himself.

"Mom!" called Barefoot. "Come see what I made." Barefoot stood up to show her the tower. *CRASH! BANG!* "Oh, no!" cried Barefoot.

"Poor Barefoot," said his mother. "You're having a bad day. Everything is going wrong. You're lucky it's almost time for bed."

Barefoot Bear put his pajamas on and sat down in front of the television set.

His mother brought him some milk and cookies. But Barefoot wasn't hungry. He put the cookies in his pocket for later.

A scary movie was on TV. A gigantic lizard was frightening people in a little town.

The lizard was called Mongo. His eyes glowed like yellow coals. Flames shot out of his mouth. And green puffs of smoke curled out of his ears. Barefoot watched, terrified, as Mongo reached down to grab a—

"Barefoot!" called his mother. "Bedtime!"
"Not now," said Barefoot. "This is the best part."
"Right now," said his father. "Bedtime."
Barefoot stomped off to bed. But he couldn't fall asleep.

Barefoot lay on his back.
He lay on his side.
He turned over two times. But still he did not fall
asleep.

"Dad!" cried Barefoot. "Can I have a glass of water?"
Barefoot's father brought him some water. Barefoot
drank it.

He lay down again. Still he couldn't fall asleep.
Scritch, scratch. Barefoot sat up in bed.
What was that noise?

Barefoot looked around his dark room. The closet door was open. Hadn't it been closed before?

And what was that glowing in the closet? Barefoot thought he saw two yellow eyes.

"Mom!" he called. "Mom! Mongo is in my closet."

Barefoot's mother came into his room. She turned on the light and opened the closet door.

"No Mongo here," she said. "Just your clothes. Go to sleep now, Barefoot. Good night."

"Good night," replied Barefoot as he closed his eyes. But still he did not feel sleepy.

Scritch, scratch. Barefoot heard the noise again. It was coming from under his bed!

"Yipes!" Barefoot curled up into a little ball. He scrunched all the way over to the other side of his bed.

He scrunched over so far that he fell onto the floor with a *THUMP*.

"Ow," said Barefoot, rubbing his elbow.

"Barefoot!" Barefoot's father ran into the room and turned on the light. "Are you all right?" he asked.

"I guess so," said Barefoot. "I fell out of bed. I thought I heard Mongo."

"Poor Barefoot," said his father. "You're having a bad day. Everything is going wrong."

His father looked under his bed. "No Mongo here," he said. Then he tucked Barefoot under the covers again.

"Dad," said Barefoot, "I can't fall asleep."

"Maybe a story would help," said his father. "Shall I read to you?"

"Okay," replied Barefoot.

Barefoot's father sat down in the rocking chair. He opened a big book of bedtime stories. "Here's a story about a princess and a big, fire-breathing dragon," he said.

Barefoot snuggled into his bed.

"Once upon a time," began Barefoot's father, "there lived a beautiful princess named Arabella. One day while she was riding her horse through the woods, she heard a sound coming from deep within a cave."

"What kind of sound, Dad?" asked Barefoot.

"A scritchy, scratchy sound," answered his father. "Arabella was curious. She got off her horse and looked into the cave."

Barefoot Bear smiled. He was feeling sleepy. His eyelids began to droop.

"*ZAP!*" read Barefoot's father. "Blinding flames shot out at Arabella. A cloud of green smoke rose up. A scaly dragon stood in front of Arabella, breathing fire."

Barefoot's father looked up from the storybook. He saw
that Barefoot was fast asleep, so he turned off the light
and tiptoed out of the room.

All of a sudden Barefoot woke up. He was in his bed,
but he was not in his room.

He was someplace dark and rocky. Barefoot shivered.
He was in a cave!

"Help!" he heard a voice cry. Someone was in trouble.

"Who's there?" called Barefoot Bear as he sat up in his bed.

"It's me, Princess Arabella. Mongo tied me up and scared my horse away."

"Mongo!" yelped Barefoot. He got to his feet. He stumbled toward the voice.

"Don't worry," said Barefoot bravely. "I'll save you."

"Please hurry," Arabella cried. "We must escape before Mongo returns."

Barefoot started to untie the rope. His paws didn't slip once. In a flash, Arabella was free.

"Oh, thank you!" she said. "You are a wonderful bear!"
Under his fur, Barefoot blushed a deep red. "Now we
must hurry and escape," said the princess. "Mongo
would like Arabella stew for dinner."

"Stew!" said Barefoot. "This way. Follow me."
Barefoot took Arabella's paw. They ran through a
passageway. They ran until Barefoot saw two yellow eyes
shining in the darkness ahead of them.

Barefoot stopped short. "What is it?" asked the princess.

"Shh," said Barefoot. "Mongo's coming."

"Oh, no! What should we do?"

"Hide," whispered Barefoot. "Over here."

Barefoot pulled Arabella behind a rock. They crouched down.

Thump, thump, thump. Mongo was coming closer. He swished his scaly tail. Sparks shot from his mouth.

When he reached the rock that was hiding Barefoot and the princess, he stopped. He sniffed the air.

Oh, no, thought Barefoot. Arabella stew . . . Barefoot stew!

Then he had an idea. He reached into his pocket
and felt for the cookies.
They were still there.

Barefoot took the cookies out. Mmm . . . nutty-chocolately-chip. Mongo sniffed the air again. Barefoot tossed the cookies far back into the cave. Mongo ran after them greedily, following the scent.

"Quick!" whispered Barefoot. "Let's go." Barefoot could see daylight ahead. He and Arabella ran out of the cave and through the woods, away from Mongo.

"We made it!" cried Arabella finally. "We're safe. You saved us, Barefoot Bear." Barefoot smiled. He felt very proud of himself.

Maybe this wasn't such a bad day after all, he thought.

Arabella's horse was grazing in a small green meadow. Barefoot looked around. He and the princess were at the edge of a forest. In the distance, he could see a castle with a tall tower.

"Come on," said Barefoot. "I'll take you home." He
jumped onto the horse and pulled Arabella up after him.
Then they galloped all the way to Arabella's castle.

Barefoot and the princess rode across a drawbridge over a moat. The king and queen were waiting in the courtyard.

"Arabella!" they shouted. Barefoot slid off the horse and helped the princess down.

Arabella ran to her parents. "Mongo captured me!" she exclaimed. "But Barefoot Bear rescued me. He saved my life!"

"What a brave and noble bear you are!" said the king. "For saving my daughter's life, I shall make you a knight. You will be Sir Barefoot."

"You are a hero," added the queen. "I shall make today
Barefoot Bear Day, in your honor."
Barefoot grinned. What a great day!

But before he could thank the king and queen, they faded away. So did Arabella and her horse. Barefoot blinked his eyes.

He was back in his very own bed.

He wasn't a knight or a hero. He was just Barefoot
Bear. Everything had gone wrong that day.

But in his dream, everything had gone right. Barefoot
had saved the day! He smiled happily. Tomorrow would
be better.

Barefoot closed his eyes. Maybe he would dream again. Maybe he would find Arabella and her horse. They would ride to her castle.

And Barefoot Bear would be Sir Barefoot . . . at least until tomorrow.